About the Author

Lois has always had a love of storytelling. She passionately believes that more than ever, children today really need the messages of kindness and consideration, helping others, forgiveness, encouragement, and pride. These are subtly conveyed throughout her writing in the spirit of great fun!

She lives with her husband by the sea in Dorset, and draws much of her inspiration from this beautiful part of the world.

www.kindiscool.co.uk

Great Grandma Joins the Circus

Lois Davis

Great Grandma Joins the Circus

Olympia Publishers
London

www.olympiapublishers.com
OLYMPIA PAPERBACK EDITION

A CIP catalogue record for this title is
available from the British Library.

ISBN: 978-1-84897-858-4

First Published in 2017

Olympia Publishers
60 Cannon Street
London
EC4N 6NP

Printed in Great Britain

Dedication

For Benji, with love

Acknowledgements

First and foremost, heartfelt thanks go to my husband Keith. Your support and faith in me has been total.

To all my family, from three to ninety-three, for your unwavering encouragement and pride, especially Benji, for his great enthusiasm and who could hardly wait for this moment!

Thanks must also go to the following people at Olympia. Max Stern, Chief Editor for believing in me. James Houghton, Executive Editor for your guidance, help, and advice. And lastly but by no means least, heartfelt thanks to Illustrator Harriat King, who has captured the essence of my storytelling and characterisations so beautifully.

Chapter 1

The poster pinned to the big oak tree by the village church read:

The Great Alfredo Macaroni and The Great Randolpho Ravioli bring the most spectacular circus show on earth to the village of Howdoyoudo a week on Saturday! Four incredible days! Please enquire for tickets and information at the Post Office counter.

Standing reading the poster, Great Grandma thought, 'Oh, how positively exciting!' Making her way without delay to the Post Office, her best friend – the postmistress, Peggy Stamper – was delighted to see her. There was a pile of leaflets about the circus on the Post Office counter. Taking one, Great Grandma could see that there was an advert to join the circus.

Clowns required. Experience essential.
Flying trapeze artist required. Training will be given.
Please apply in person at the main tent on the village green.

Saying goodbye to Peggy and leaving the Post Office, Great Grandma crossed the bridge over the railway line. The 10.42 from Jelly Junction was coming down the track at tremendous speed, whistling loudly. Great Grandma was deep in thought, and the noise made her jump! Approaching the village green, she could see a line of people queuing up by the entrance to the main tent. Joining the line, she soon found herself at the head of the queue.

"Next, please," boomed a voice from inside the tent.

Great Grandma stepped inside. At a table sat The Great Alfredo Macaroni and The Great Randolpho Ravioli. They both had the longest, most twirly moustaches that Great Grandma had ever seen!

In a deep voice that seemed to come from his boots, Alfredo spoke first. "Good morning, madam."

"And how may we help you?" continued Randolpho.

"Good morning, gentlemen," replied Great Grandma. "I see you have a vacancy for a flying trapeze artist for the circus."

"Indeed, we do," Alfredo answered. "Please, tell us why you have applied."

"Well, I have always dreamt of flying through the air on a trapeze, but I have never had the opportunity before to join a circus. I don't weigh very much and I am very fit," replied Great Grandma.

Alfredo and Randolpho turned to look at each other. For all the people they had seen that morning, they had never seen a little old lady applying to be a flying trapeze artist! Looking back at Great Grandma, they both spoke at the same time.

"We'll let you know by tomorrow," they said.

Leaving the tent, Great Grandma hoped so much they would choose her from all the other people applying. Putting the leaflet that she had picked up in the Post Office safely in her handbag and crossing back over the railway bridge, she waited for the bus home.

Meanwhile, Mincemeat, Great Grandma's very large and exceptionally furry lovely ginger cat, was in the garden hanging washing on the line as Great Grandma returned home.

Mincemeat, who adored cooking, had just put a roast dandelion and snail pie topped with mashed potatoes, in the oven to be ready for lunch. Still wearing his 'I Love Cooking' apron, he fished about in his apron pocket for the last of the pegs to hang up Great Grandma's long red-and-white stripy socks.

"Did you have a good morning, Great Grandma?" Mincemeat enquired.

"Oh, nothing out of the ordinary," she replied.

"Well, lunch is nearly ready," he said. "I've made one of your favourites."

Great Grandma thoroughly enjoyed the roast dandelion and snail pie, but Mincemeat thought she looked sleepy.

"You look tired, Great Grandma. I'll clear up here. Go and have a rest in the sitting room. I won't disturb you. I'll be out in the shed. I thought I'd take my motorbike to bits this afternoon and give the engine a good clean. I'm sure it needs oiling."

"I think I will, if you don't mind, Mincemeat. I do feel quite tired," she replied.

Settling herself on the sofa, Great Grandma was soon sound asleep, dreaming of becoming a world famous flying trapeze artist in The Great Alfredo Macaroni and The Great Randolpho Ravioli's most spectacular circus show on earth!

Chapter 2

Joe Parcel It Up, the village postman, came round to the back kitchen door next morning as usual. Putting the post on the kitchen table, he stopped – as he often did – to have a cup of tea, always hopeful there would be something freshly baked to go with it! Today was no exception, as Mincemeat, putting on his oven gloves was just taking some meltingly delicious toffee shortbread biscuits out of the oven.

"Good morning, Joe, perfect timing," said Mincemeat. "I'll put the kettle on."

Chatting away, Mincemeat didn't look at the post that Joe had brought. As the grandfather clock in the hall struck eleven, Mincemeat suddenly realized he had to be in the village for a dental appointment.

"I'm sorry, Joe, I really have to go or I'll be late! I have a dental check-up with Geronimo Gum."

"And I'll be in trouble with Peggy Stamper if I don't get a move on!" said Joe.

Saying goodbye, Joe carried on his post round, as Mincemeat ran down the hill for the next bus into the village. Percy Crabapple was just rounding the corner in Roast Potato Lane in his bus, as Mincemeat, waving madly at Percy to stop, reached the bus stop.

Great Grandma had been out all morning visiting Rose Petal, who needed some help weeding her garden. Arriving home, she put her handbag down on the kitchen table. Seeing the pile of post, her gaze fell on a white envelope with the initials 'AM' and 'RR' in the top left-hand corner of the envelope.

Great Grandma's heart skipped a beat, as gingerly, she opened the letter.

'*Dear Great Grandma,*' the letter began.

'*After careful consideration, The Great Alfredo Macaroni and The Great Randolpho Ravioli...*

(She could hardly dare to read on!)

... are delighted to offer you an audition to become a flying trapeze artist for our circus! Please report to the main tent on the village green tomorrow morning at ten o'clock.'

Great Grandma had a feeling like butterflies in her tummy, as a wave of excitement came over her as she thought about becoming a flying trapeze artist!

There was a poster in the dental surgery about the circus coming to the village. Seeing the two advertisements for vacancies for clowns and the flying trapeze artist, Mincemeat thought how brave someone must be to become a flying trapeze artist! Although he was a magic cat and could fly through the air himself, he couldn't imagine flying as high as a trapeze artist! In any event, Great Grandma had always told him not to fly higher than the washing line! He had only ever flown around the cottage garden, apart from his adventure to Australia, but that's another story!

That evening over supper, Mincemeat said, "There was a poster in the dental surgery today, Great Grandma, about a circus coming to the village. Would you like to go? I can get tickets if you like."

Great Grandma nearly choked on her beetle squash!

Coughing and clearing her throat, she said, "You go ahead, Mincemeat. I'm feeling rather tired these days. Why don't you ask Rose Petal? I was there this morning visiting her, helping her with her weeding. I'm sure she'd be delighted to go with you."

"Oh, well, if you're sure, Great Grandma. I would like to go. Yes, I'll ask Rose. She doesn't get out much. Do you know, they are advertising for clowns and a flying trapeze artist!"

"Really!" exclaimed Great Grandma. "Well, I never!"

Chapter 3

The huge trucks reversed onto the village green, shuddering to a halt beside each other. The Big Top circus tent was going up! Making her way to the main tent as the letter had requested, Great Grandma felt the thrill of the activity all around her! People on stilts were practising. They seemed as tall as the trees to Great Grandma who was really not very tall herself. A man on a unicycle – a bicycle with only one wheel – sped past Great Grandma. She was astounded that he could balance without falling off! Jugglers juggled, and a group of children practised handstands. There were several clowns larking about and a flying custard pie just missed Great Grandma as she reached the tent! Going inside, a troupe of acrobats were somersaulting from one side to the other.

A man in a black top hat, wearing a red waistcoat and holding a clipboard greeted Great Grandma. "Good morning. I am Geraldo Gelati, the Ring Master. I am delighted to meet you, Madam. You must be Great Grandma. I have you on my list here that you are auditioning to be our flying trapeze artist."

"That's right, Mr Gelati. I am very pleased to meet you too."

"Oh, please, call me Geraldo," he replied. "After your audition, I will decide if you have been successful. Let's get started then."

"Oh, how thrilling!" remarked Great Grandma. "I brought my own safety net," she replied, fishing about in her hand bag to retrieve it.

"Splendissimo!" Geraldo Gelati declared.

Putting on a safety harness, Great Grandma's heart flipped as she climbed the ladder up to the platform. Reaching the top, she stepped onto the platform before gripping the bar launching herself into mid-air!

"I'm flying, Geraldo!" she shrieked. "I'm flying!"

"Bravo, bravo! That will do. Please come down," Geraldo called back.

Descending the ladder, Great Grandma could see below her a tightrope walker wearing a sparkly pink leotard practising her act. A man practising plate spinning was spinning plates on top of a line of poles. Running down the line, he spun plate after plate, although every now and then there was a huge crash as one spun off the pole and onto the floor!

"I am very happy to tell you, Great Grandma, that training will start immediately, and you will need to be here to practise every day all next week until the day before the circus opens."

By the end of the following week, Great Grandma was ready for the opening night of the circus. She could now fly through the air effortlessly, and she loved every minute of it.

Chapter 4

In Fieldmouse Meadows, Great Grandma's Aunt Petunia was reversing her pumpkin car out of her garage. Aunt Petunia and her best friend Lavinia Honeybun had bought tickets for the circus. Great Grandma had no idea that her aunt would be in the audience.

Mincemeat, meanwhile, was putting on his best orange waistcoat that he kept for special occasions. He had arranged to pick up Rose Petal at six o'clock that evening. Great Grandma was out and hadn't returned home yet, so leaving a note in his rather wiggly writing for her on the kitchen table, he then closed the kitchen door behind him.

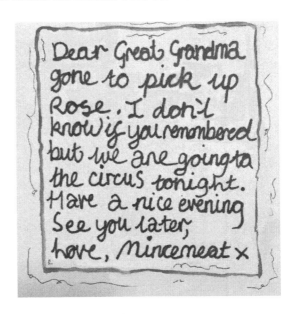

Dear Great Grandma
gone to pick up
Rose. I don't
know if you remembered
but we are going to
the circus tonight.
Have a nice evening
See you later,
love, Mincemeat x

Steering his motorbike out of the shed and putting on his crash helmet and black spotted motorbike rider's suit, Mincemeat drove down the hill and out into the lane to pick up Rose.

"You look beautiful, Rose," said Mincemeat as Rose Petal answered the door.

"Thank you, Mincemeat. This is so exciting! I haven't been to the circus for such a long time."

"Me neither," replied Mincemeat, helping Rose into the sidecar.

Approaching the village green, wonderful music could be heard from the Big Top circus tent. A band was playing. Cymbals were crashing, loud trumpets sounded, there was an instrument that made a whistling noise, flutes played and drums went boom, boom!

Parking his motor bike and helping Rose out of the sidecar, Mincemeat and Rose walked towards the Big Top. Showing their tickets to the usherette, they settled themselves in their seats. Mincemeat had managed to get front row seats with a splendid view of the whole arena. The tent was filling up, and soon there was not a seat to be had. A hum of excitement filled the air.

Suddenly, Mincemeat felt a tap on his shoulder.

"Mincemeat, what a surprise to see you! Where's Great Grandma?" It was Aunt Petunia.

"Oh, how lovely to see you, Aunt Petunia. This is my friend, Rose Petal, by the way. Great Grandma was feeling rather tired, so she didn't come with us."

"Oh, that's a shame. This is my best friend, Lavinia Honeybun, Rose." Turning to Lavinia, Aunt Petunia said, "You remember Mincemeat, don't you, dear?"

"Indeed, I do, especially his wonderful baking! I'm very pleased to meet you, Rose. We had better find our seats. I think it's going to start shortly. Bye, see you soon."

Suddenly the lights dimmed right down, and there was a drum roll as into the ring came The Great Alfredo Macaroni and The Great Randolpho Ravioli, the spotlight on them. Over the loudspeakers, they welcomed the crowd.

"Good evening, ladies, gentlemen, and children!" said Randolpho Ravioli, his voice echoing out over the tannoy.

"We are delighted to welcome you all here tonight!" continued Alfredo Macaroni. "Please give a big hand to your ring master, Geraldo Gelati!"

Striding out into the centre of the ring and standing under the spotlight, Geraldo Gelati took a deep bow as the whole tent erupted in applause.

The first act on was Hercules. Geraldo Gelati's voice came over the loudspeaker.

"Ladies, gentlemen, and children, please give a warm welcome to Hercules – the world's one and only weightlifting hamster!"

The crowd clapped hard, and as the applause died down, a circus assistant brought a barbell onto the centre of the arena. Hercules followed. He was wearing a black waistcoat decorated with very glittery silver sequins together with a matching bow tie.

The spotlight centred on Hercules as he took a long slow bow. There was complete hush from the audience. Positioning himself in front of the barbell, he steadied himself with both feet, staring straight ahead. Taking a deep breath and puffing out his chest, he continued to stand quite still for a moment. Then, bending forward and gripping each end of the barbell, he lifted it high above his head. The crowd roared and cheered!

As Hercules left the arena, a whole group of clowns wearing big red noses, baggy trousers and huge shoes, came running out. Carrying buckets full to the top of what appeared to be water, they began running around the arena throwing the contents over the seated crowd! As people ducked preparing to get soaked, they realised that the buckets were actually full of hundreds of silver streamers! The people were amazed, and everybody laughed.

Very cheekily, the clowns who wore big floppy bow ties, then moved between the rows of seats to say hello, shaking hands with people as they went. There was great surprise amongst the crowd as this time they did get wet! The bow ties squirted out a shower of water! The clowns had great fun spraying everybody they could!

Aunt Petunia and Lavinia Honeybun squealed as they got sprayed! Then, one of the clowns ran off to get a small table, placing it in the centre of the arena. On it was a bright orange cloth, plates, bowls and cutlery.

The band struck up a drum roll as another clown grasped two corners of the cloth quickly pulling it towards him, leaving all the plates, bowls and cutlery still on the table as he did so! Everybody clapped loudly. Picking up the table to show the crowd, they could see that everything on the table was actually attached with string! The audience roared with laughter!

Turning to Rose Petal, Mincemeat said, "I don't think I'd better try that at home!"

The lights brightening, it was time for the interval. Long queues were forming for ice-cream. Mincemeat went to find where Aunt Petunia and Lavinia Honeybun were sitting to ask if they would like an ice-cream.

"That's very kind of you, Mincemeat. What would you like, Lavinia?" asked Aunt Petunia.

"Cherry and chocolate, please," replied Lavinia.

"I'll have the same, please, Mincemeat, thank you very much."

Mincemeat went off to queue for four ice-creams, not so sure how he was going to carry them all. Rose Petal had asked for vanilla and nettle, and Mincemeat fancied one of his favourites – shrimp and sardine flavour! Soon, reaching the head of the queue, he then carefully manoeuvred himself back to Rose Petal and to where Aunt Petunia and Lavinia were sitting, without dropping a single ice-cream!

"Well done, Mincemeat!" said Aunt Petunia. "Thank you. What a great shame Great Grandma didn't feel able to come to watch the circus. I'm sure she would have enjoyed it."

"Yes, it is a shame, but I'll certainly be able to tell her all about it when I get home," replied Mincemeat.

Making his way back to his seat next to Rose Petal, he was just in time to get settled for the second half of the show whilst enjoying his ice-cream, as the lights dimmed again.

Chapter 5

Geraldo Gelati once more strode out into the centre of the arena and stood under the spotlight.

"Ladies, gentlemen, and children, never seen before and performing for the first time in The Great Alfredo Macaroni and The Great Randolpho Ravioli's Big Top circus, is a new flying trapeze artist! Please, put your hands together to welcome the one, the only, flying Great Grandma!"

Mincemeat dropped his ice-cream!

In the darkened circus tent, the only light now, was a spotlight centred high above the floor on a tiny figure above. Taking hold of the trapeze bar, dressed in a green-and-white striped leotard with purple leggings, Great Grandma stood for a moment before propelling herself off the platform flying into the air. Shrieking with laughter, she flew from one side of the platform to the other and back again several times.

Down below, Mincemeat sat stunned. He could not believe his eyes. Equally open-mouthed was Aunt Petunia. Turning to Lavinia Honeybun beside her, she said, "Never in all my life have I seen such a thing! Whoever would have thought it!"

High above their heads, as she reached the end of her performance, Great Grandma waved to the crowd below. They waved back, standing to applaud her.

Leaving his seat, and taking Rose Petal with him, Mincemeat headed round to the performers' entrance at the back of the tent. It wasn't long before Great Grandma emerged.

"Was that really you, Great Grandma?" asked Mincemeat as soon as he saw her.

"Indeed, it was, Mincemeat, indeed, it was!" replied Great Grandma.

They were now joined by Aunt Petunia and Lavinia Honeybun. Everybody was chattering at once, saying how they couldn't believe their eyes, or the fact that Great Grandma had kept such a secret! Great Grandma, thoroughly enjoying all the fuss just stood and smiled! Amid all the chattering, it was decided that Rose, Aunt Petunia and Lavinia should all have supper at Great Grandma and Mincemeat's cottage that evening. Loving food as he did, Mincemeat always had the freezer well stocked! Aunt Petunia gave Great Grandma a lift in her car with Lavinia. Arriving home with Rose, Mincemeat pulled out a large juicy meat and dumpling pie from the freezer and a lavender-flavoured rice pudding. Aunt Petunia wanted to know if Great Grandma was actually going to join the circus as their flying trapeze artist and tour the world!

"Oh, no, I'm far too old for that, and I couldn't possibly be away from Mincemeat. But I'm glad I did it, very glad," she said rather sleepily.

Supper over, Aunt Petunia and Lavinia could see that Great Grandma was very tired so they said their goodbyes.

"We must all get together again soon, dear," Aunt Petunia said to Great Grandma. "Perhaps you'll come out to Fieldmouse Meadows with Mincemeat and Rose."

"Thank you, that's a lovely idea," replied Great Grandma.

Helping Mincemeat clear away all the dishes, Rose said she really should be getting home.

Great Grandma had already said goodnight and was fast asleep in bed dreaming of her wonderful day, as Mincemeat took Rose home in the sidecar of his motorbike.

Coming downstairs the next morning to make Great Grandma a cup of tea as usual, Mincemeat saw that the morning paper, The Howdoyoudo Times had already been delivered. Bending down to pick it up from the front door mat, he unfolded it. There, on the very front page was the headline:

Star of the show! Queen of the circus! The one, the only, Great Grandma, flying trapeze artist wowed the crowds with her amazing, astonishing performance last night!

Below the headline, was a large photograph of The Great Alfredo Macaroni and The Great Randolpho Ravioli towering over Great Grandma as she stood between them smiling broadly.

Tears sprang into Mincemeat's eyes. He truly felt he had never been so proud in all his life.

THE HOWDOYOUDO TIMES

MONDAY 16th JUNE

'STAR of the show'

'QUEEN OF THE CIRCUS!'

49226776R00022

Made in the USA
Middletown, DE
19 June 2019